Life in Numbers

Smart Shoppers

Karin Anderson, M.A.T.

Publishing Credits

Rachelle Cracchiolo, M.S.Ed., *Publisher*
Conni Medina, M.A.Ed., *Managing Editor*
Nika Fabienke, Ed.D., *Series Developer*
June Kikuchi, *Content Director*
John Leach, *Assistant Editor*
Kevin Pham, *Graphic Designer*

Image Credits: front cover, p.1 Tooykrub/Shutterstock; p.16 jfmdesign/iStock; p.23 second from top: Kunal Mehta/Shutterstock.com; all other images from iStock and/or Shutterstock.

Library of Congress Cataloging-in-Publication Data

Names: Anderson, Karin, author.
Title: Life in numbers : smart shoppers / Karin Anderson, M.A.T.
Description: Huntington Beach, CA : Teacher Created Materials, [2018] | Audience: K to grade 3.
Identifiers: LCCN 2017026879 (print) | LCCN 2017054042 (ebook) | ISBN 9781425853303 (eBook) | ISBN 9781425849566 (pbk.)
Subjects: LCSH: Shopping--Juvenile literature.
Classification: LCC TX335.5 (ebook) | LCC TX335.5 .A53 2018 (print) | DDC 640.73--dc23
LC record available at https://lccn.loc.gov/2017026879

Teacher Created Materials
5301 Oceanus Drive
Huntington Beach, CA 92649-1030
http://www.tcmpub.com

ISBN 978-1-4258-4956-6

Printed in China WAI002

We shop at a grocery store! We choose what to buy.

We need a cart. Should we get a small **basket** or a big cart?

I choose the big cart.

We need fruit.
Mom asks, "Should we buy apples or pears?"

I choose both. We buy three apples and five pears.

We need carrots. "Should we buy big or small carrots?" asks Mom.

I choose eight small carrots.

We need eggs. Here are twelve eggs.

Here are six eggs. We choose twelve eggs.

We have money left for one treat!

I choose ice cream!

We had fun shopping.

We made many choices.

Glossary

basket

choices

grocery store

shopping